Going to Press

THE OPPORTUNITY

Going to Press

D. M. PAIGE

darbycreek

Darby Creek
A division of Lerner Publishing Group, Inc.
241 First Avenue North
Minneapolis, MN 55401 U.S.A.

Website address: www.lernerbooks.com

Cover and interior photographs © DreamPictures/Blend Images/Getty Images (girl); © iStockphoto.com/Jordan McCullough (title texture).

Main body text set in Janson Text LT Std 12/17.
Typeface provided by Linotype AG.

The Cataloging-in-Publication Data for *Going to Press* is on file at the Library of Congress.
ISBN: 978–1–4677–1373–3 (LB)
ISBN: 978–1–4677–1674–1 (EB)

Manufactured in the United States of America
1 – SB – 7/15/13

In order to succeed, your desire for success should be greater than your fear of failure.

—Bill Cosby

PROLOGUE

Dear Ms. Harris,

Who? Lisa Harris

What? A prestigious internship at *The Rage*, America's premier music magazine. All expenses paid.

When? Summer 2014

Where? New York City

How? You are invited to be part of the Harmon Holt internship program

Why? Because of your work as editor-in-chief of Clinton High's newspaper, *The Blaze*, your exemplary writing skills, and your high GPA

It is my pleasure to welcome you, Lisa.

It may be hard to see it now, but the distance between me and you is hard work and opportunity. I am giving you the opportunity. The rest is up to you.

Sincerely,
Harmon Holt

ONE

"Do it again," I demanded, circling another typo with red ink and handing it back to Harmony. Harmony's bottom lip trembled a little bit as she looked at the paper and then back at me. "I asked for a thousand words on the new cheerleading team, and you gave me five hundred." I was tempted to backtrack because of the look on her face, but I needed the story yesterday and she hadn't delivered.

Harmony walked away, head down, and back to her computer.

"Do you have to be so mean about it?" asked

Jason Morgan.

I looked up at him, surprised. He was good at his job—sports photography—and he covered an area that I knew nothing about. I opened my mouth to explain that this paper and everything in it was important to me. There was a reason I spent hours poring over my articles before they went to press. There was a reason I never trusted spell-check or Wikipedia. If it wasn't good enough, then I would never get a scholarship, go to college, or get a job in journalism. One grammatical error, one incorrect fact, and I could be looking at a different career path. All I could say was, "I just like things done right."

"You can catch more Harmonys with honey," he quipped before looking back at his screen. It was filled with pictures from the basketball team's last big game. They lost, but it was a superclose call.

I looked back at the computer. I had new mail.

Dear Ms. Harris, . . . You are invited to be part of the Harmon Holt internship program.

I screamed.

"What is it now?" Jason asked. "Did someone not use enough commas?"

I rolled my eyes at him, but I couldn't even manage to frown. I had no one else to tell.

"I just got an internship at *The Rage*!"

TWO

A week later I was standing in New York City in front of the NYU dorm where I would be staying and living out my dream to be a reporter.

Harmon Holt's assistant carried my one bag to my room. I wasn't expecting such personal treatment from the billionaire media mogul, but it made him that much cooler in my imagination.

The room was small—just a bed and a desk. But just outside my window was Union Square, a little park surrounded by shops and restaurants. A farmer's market was filled with people on one side. This was the kind of New York scene that I had imagined my whole life.

The room was a single. No roommate. I wanted to be all about my internship, no distractions. So this was good, right? But right this second I wished I had someone to tell about my view and gush to about how excited I was for my internship.

"So, will I get to meet Mr. Holt soon? I'd really like to thank him," I said.

The assistant shook his head. "Unlikely. Mr. Holt takes a keen interest in the interns. But he is also a very busy man. He'll get regular reports from your supervisors. But I doubt you'll get to meet in person. You might, though, want to write him a note when the internship is over. He likes that."

As the assistant made for the door, he gave me his card and asked me if I needed anything.

"No, this is perfect."

"I'm sure your friends at school can't wait to hear all about the big city," he said.

"Um . . ." The truth was that I didn't really have any friends back home. I was always so busy with school and the paper. Friends just didn't happen. Not really. "Yeah, they can't wait."

He said good-bye and was gone.

I pulled my phone out of my pocket and took a picture of my amazing view. I wished I could call my dad, but he wasn't supposed to take calls while he was driving his cab, so I texted the picture instead. Under it I wrote, *I made it Dad! :)*

THREE

When I walked into the *Rage* office, I realized right away I was overdressed.

I was wearing a pair of slacks, a blouse, and heels. Everyone else was dressed like they were ready to go to a concert. Denim, leather, graphic tees, motorcycle boots . . . not one button-down in sight. I looked like a schoolgirl in sea of cool, rock n' roll types. I scanned the modern newsroom, where reporters sat in supermodern egg-shaped chairs in cubicles made of red, blue, and yellow plastic.

A girl with a honey-colored Afro and a dress

over jeggings led me down the hall, which was wallpapered with *Rage* covers. I'd read most of them. There were pictures of hip-hop and rock stars on every cover. Beyoncé, Prince, the Rolling Stones, J.Lo, the list went on and on. It was like a wall of cool.

"I'm Tam, Holiday's assistant. I usually handle all the intern stuff. I'll get you started."

I nodded. For once short on words.

Tam must have sensed my nerves. "Don't worry, honey. She's going to love you," she said.

Was I going to fit in here? I should have checked out their dress code. I'd reread the last five issues cover to cover. I'd thought of clever things to say about the latest issue. But I never thought about what I should wear. I tried to put my wardrobe malfunction thoughts away and not let my flowery blouse get in the way of the fact that I was working for *The Rage* for the whole summer!

She set me up at the intern desk in a tiny corner of the office, near the coffee room. There was a computer with a screen saver of *The Rage*'s logo bouncing around in black space.

"Holiday's got meetings until four. But you'll meet her then. In the meantime, let's get you started," she said. "Everyone here starts with fact-checking. It reminds us that everything we do here starts and ends with the truth." She picked up a big binder and handed it to me. "This is the mock-up of the issue that's going to press today. You can start by practicing with this." She handed me a highlighter and a pen.

I nodded. This I could do.

"Check every date, every spelling of every name, every fact. Start with the Internet, but stay away from Wikipedia. Only use verifiable sources like the AP. And if you can't find it here, go to the source directly." She pointed to the phone. "Then write down exactly where you got the info here." She touched the computer and it came to life. A fact-checking grid came up. "Got it?"

I nodded again.

She pointed to the binder again. "You won't find any mistakes in there. But I want to see what you can do before I give you some new articles to work on. I'll be back to check on you in about an hour." She strutted back to her desk.

I cracked open the book carefully. My very first assignment.

Even though Tam had said the proof was mistake-free, about an hour later, I found something

I picked up the binder and brought it to Tam's desk.

"What is it, hon?"

"I think I found something."

FOUR

Tam knocked on the door of Holiday Martin's office and then opened it. Inside, the editor in chief was wearing silver Converse, jeans, and a welcoming smile. She looked busy, but not too busy for her assistant. I liked her immediately. There was a girl sitting next to her desk who couldn't have been much older than twenty-five. She rolled her eyes, looking annoyed by the interruption.

"I'm sorry to interrupt, Holiday, but you have to see this. Our new intern found it," said Tam. She put the binder on Holiday's desk, open to the "Letter from the Editor" page. Tam touched my shoulder, prompting me to speak.

"It says that your first concert was Michael Jackson's *Thriller*. But it had to be his next concert tour, *Bad*, because the year is 1987."

"You're right. How did everyone miss this?"

"I'm sorry," said Tam.

Holiday shook her head. "It's not your fault, Tam. We have a whole department. I guess no one checks the editor in chief's letter." Holiday trained her eyes on me.

"Good work, Lisa."

Holiday Martin knew my name.

"Harmon says you're the next Naomi Jax, so it's fitting for you to meet the original one," Holiday said, gesturing to the girl sitting next to her.

Naomi Jax was like a rock star herself. She'd interviewed everyone from the president to Nicki Minaj. She got to travel all around the world to interview people and write stories. I wanted to grow up and have a career like hers. Naomi smiled broadly and shook my hand.

I gushed. "I am such a big fan. I've read all your work. That piece you wrote on the Sudan was life-changing." Before I'd read it, I didn't know that kids fought in wars. By the time I got to the end of the four pages, complete with pictures of little kids carrying guns, there were tears all over it.

"Thanks, it's my favorite piece," she said with a smile. She seemed to soften a little.

Holiday's face lit up like she'd just thought of something really brilliant. "I'm so happy that you two are hitting it off, because you will be spending a lot of time together. Naomi, Lisa's going to spend a week shadowing you as you write your next story."

FIVE

“So, spill it,” Naomi’s smile turned into a frown. Maybe she wasn’t happy to have me as her shadow after all. “Whose kid are you?”

We were back in the hall, and Naomi was walking fast. “Excuse me?” I stammered.

“You must be related to someone,” she continued. “The editor in chief actually told me to be nice, and she wasn’t joking, so you must be somebody’s kid. Somebody the editor actually likes.”

I shrugged. “I’m Jimmy Harris’s kid from D.C.”

She frowned, revealing deep creases in her forehead. She must frown all the time. I could tell I wasn't giving her the answer she wanted, and for some reason it felt good to keep her from having it. I got what she was getting at—that maybe I was getting special treatment because of Harmon Holt, a graduate of my high school. Harmon got me through the door. But I didn't think I'd be here if I hadn't spent the past three years working every spare minute on my school's paper.

"You get to be my shadow for the next week, yay!" I'd never heard a "yay" so forced before. She was not at all pleased. "I get the assignment from hell, but I get you as the icing on the cake." She rolled her eyes. "Thank you, Holiday. Look, kid, it's not you—you didn't ask for this. I just hate getting fluff assignments. But I have to write them so that I can write the stuff that I want to write."

"What's the assignment?"

"A puff piece on the Side Effects. We've got a *week* of interviews with them," she said, as if she was talking about something on the bottom of her shoe. The Side Effects was the hottest band in the whole country.

SIX

Outside, we raced past a line of people waiting to hail cabs and down the block to the subway. Naomi swiped her Metro card twice. I followed her through the turnstile. She informed me that we were meeting the boys at their penthouse suite in the Mandarin, a hotel that overlooked Columbus Circle.

While I struggled to keep my balance as the 1 train rumbled uptown, Naomi explained what was wrong with interviewing the Side Effects. "I could write the whole thing without even meeting them," she quipped. I wasn't convinced.

As we got out the subway, she handed me an iPad. "Use this. Take notes."

"Thanks! I'll give it right back."

"No, keep it," she shot back. "It's a spare. The office already got me the new one. And I still use a recorder anyway."

When we got there, the boys were already sitting in the living room of their lavish penthouse. They were cuter in person. Just being in the same room as the band made my heart speed up. I'd never met anyone famous before. They weren't like other boy bands to me. I liked that they all didn't look the same. Superproducer Ari Singer had done a talent search, picking out these five boys from hundreds all over the world.

Liam James, one of the lead singers, was British.

Henry Blue, the other lead singer, was African American and from the Bronx.

Manny G. was the band's drummer. He was from Mexico.

Cameron Madison played bass. He was a surfer from California.

And Hu was from Japan and played lead guitar.

They were fifteen when they started—just a bunch of nobodies. Now they were seventeen, and they were always topping the charts. But Naomi was right about the interview—she could have written it without even showing up. The boys took turns answering questions. It seemed like they'd done it a million times before. Like it was a script.

But she was wrong about something else. Even though the answers were canned, I didn't find the boys boring at all. They had that star quality people always talk about. Maybe it was the confidence that came with being good at something. At being famous. Maybe it was the hundreds of screaming girls outside the hotel. Maybe it was the millions of screaming girls around the world. Maybe it was because each boy was cuter than the next. But I felt myself leaning toward them, like they were magnetic. My iPad, the one I was supposed to writing observations on, fell to the ground.

A second later, Henry Blue was picking it up for me. When he handed it to me, our hands touched. My mouth opened to thank him, but nothing came out.

He laughed, like he was used to having girls forget how to speak in front of him. He took his place back on the couch.

Naomi, who had witnessed the whole thing, stared at me. Either she was trying to give me a chance to make up for it, or she wanted to see me fail more. But she finally introduced me to the guys.

"This is Lisa. She's my intern. Lisa, do you have any questions for the Side Effects?"

I paused and bit my lip. Every one of the boys was looking at me. Liam, the lead singer, sniggered under his breath like this interview was finally getting interesting for him. The other boys joined in the laughter, except the one who had just touched my hand. Maybe he felt something too.

I shrugged it off. That was ridiculous. He was a world-class rock star. I was a normal high school student from D.C. I racked my brain, thinking of everything I'd ever read or heard about the Side Effects. I *had* to come up with a good question. Not only to impress the guys, but also to prove my potential as a journalist to Naomi.

"Going once, going twice . . ." Liam said. He began to get up, but Henry waved him down.

I found my voice. "You guys are missing out on a lot to be who you are. Like prom and school and all the normal kid things. Is it worth it?"

Liam perked up. "Are you asking us to prom?"

The other boys laughed. I was shocked. Henry smiled again, and it put me at ease. "I'll take this one," he volunteered. "Yeah, our classroom is us camped out in front of our laptops on the tour bus. We don't get to go to football games or eat in the cafeteria or hang out with friends on the weekends . . . well, besides each other, of course. . . . But where we are now—that just can't be beat. We have been dreaming of this opportunity forever. And we don't have to wait 'til we grow up. We're doing it right now. So yeah, it's a tradeoff. I miss my mom's cooking, my little brother, and my friends back home. But this . . ."

He looked around at his bandmates and at then at the view of Columbus Circle out the window. "This doesn't happen every day. I could have gone my whole life wishing and dreaming. But we got our chance now, and we had to take it. Who knows if it would have come around again?"

Naomi smiled at me like my question had sparked one of her own. *Awesome*, I thought, *I've made an impression.* "I have one last question. You all come from different places and different backgrounds. You all say that it feels like you're brothers now, but you were put together by a manager. And like most bands—the Backstreet Boys, New Kids on the Block, TLC— you don't have a long shelf life. When the band finally does break up, where do you see yourselves going? Will you stay in music or pursue other interests? And will you keep in touch?"

The boys looked at each other, clearly not expecting such a hard-hitting question. I could feel the manager quietly seething with rage.

Liam got up and stormed off. The others followed—all except Henry. His dark brown eyes were looking at me when he answered. He sighed. "The Side Effects isn't just another boy band. We hope to stay together for as long as this ride takes us. And if it's ever over, we hope we'll still be making music. But we'll always be brothers, 'cause there's no one else on earth who went through this with us. No one else can understand what it's like."

With that, he walked away.

Naomi nodded and we gathered our things.

The manager stepped in, not pleased. "If you pull something like that again, we're killing the rest of your access."

"No you're not—your boys need this story. Either I run it with the cover caption 'Long Live the Side Effects,' or I run it with 'Is this the Beginning of The End?' Your choice."

I gulped. Naomi was blackmailing the manager. I thought that kind of thing only happened in soap operas—the kind that I caught Dad watching during the day when he was on break from an overnight shift.

The manager blinked and handed Naomi the band's schedule for the rest of the week. I stayed quiet. We certainly hadn't covered this one in journalism class.

SEVEN

The next day, I met Naomi at the recording studio.

It looked just like I'd seen on those MTV specials when they follow a band into a recording room or on a music video shoot and you get to see all the band members goof off with one another. I was excited to see the guys in their element.

There was a big sound-mixing board in one room and a sound guy sitting behind it, mixing and adjusting what was being recorded on the other side of the glass wall. The band was all sitting on stools. No dance moves. No matching outfits. No girls dancing behind them. This was more serious than I'd expected. It was refreshing.

"It's an a cappella version of their biggest hit, 'Love Me like a Star,'" the sound guy said.

"They really can sing," I said out loud.

"If only they had something to say," Naomi muttered under her breath.

She was right. Their songs so far hadn't exactly been deep . . . but they *were* catchy—the kind of songs you hum in the shower and while you're doing homework. The kind of songs you just can't shake once you know the melody.

After they were done, I expected Naomi to ask them questions, but she just waved at them and began to walk out.

"Aren't we going to talk to them?" I asked.

"Tomorrow at the party. Sometimes it's good to just observe them in their comfort zone. Plus, they're giving me nothing. They don't argue. They agree about everything. They don't get any bad press."

"And that's a bad thing?"

"If there's no passion, do they even really care?"

She pulled out her iPad and began writing something. Probably the mean thing she'd just said about them. Then she pushed her way out of the studio and began taking the stairs two by two. I followed her.

"Go, see the city. I'm going to get a massage," Naomi announced and rushed off. Within seconds she had disappeared into the crush of people on the sidewalk. I took a few steps before realizing I had left my iPad on one of the chairs next to the sound board. I ran back upstairs.

When I got back to the studio, Henry was singing in the sound booth alone. I touched the button on the sound board that I'd seen the sound guy hit so that Henry's voice filled the room. It wasn't the normal hip-hop crossover pop stuff that I had heard before. It was deeper and slower, a real love song.

I was impressed. He spotted me through the glass and stopped singing. I picked up my tablet and waved it in the air to show him that I hadn't come back to spy on him and then began to make my way out.

When I was walking back down the steps, Henry caught up with me. "Hey, wait up!" he said.

"I liked the song. It's different from what you guys normally sing."

"Thanks."

He held the door open for me.

"I liked your question."

I raised my eyebrows. It was his job to charm teenage girls.

"Everyone assumes that we don't miss the other stuff, the real stuff." He sounded sincere.

"I go to a normal school and get to be a normal girl, but I still feel like I'm missing out on stuff." I wanted to take the words back as soon as I said them. I'd just compared my little life to his big one. But he nodded as if we were totally the same.

An SUV pulled up in front of the building with the rest of the band already inside.

"There you are, loser. Hop in," Liam demanded.

"Can we drop you somewhere?" Henry asked.

One of the other boys mimicked him, "Can we drop you—" Someone else stopped him—it sounded like Cameron's surfer-boy accent: "Stop stepping on his game, man."

"That's not game," Manny said, drumming his hands against the back of a seat.

"I'm good," I said, letting him off the hook.

He slid into the back of the SUV, and I watched as it pulled away from the curb.

Was Henry of the Side Effects really flirting with me? It couldn't be possible.

The window rolled down as I started to walk away.

"You should totally come to our rehearsal later. Your reporter mom isn't invited."

"You totally should," added another voice from behind him.

"Should she?" Liam said, with a big pout that I'd never seen in any of their interviews or videos.

"Okay . . . sure," I stuttered.

"Awesome. The manager will text you with

the deets." The window rolled up, and the SUV disappeared into traffic. I walked all the way back to my dorm, but I was daydreaming so much, I barely saw a thing.

EIGHT

When I got back to my dorm, I remembered something. Or, rather, someone . . . Naomi. She would kill me when she found out I'd said yes to Henry's invitation. Maybe I shouldn't have said yes. Did that cross some line? Had I stepped on her interview? Had I stepped on her story? I had to tell her. I called her, and she answered on the first ring, "Hello, intern. This better be good."

I told her almost everything, but I left out the part about the new song. Somehow it seemed private. I wanted to keep it between just me and Henry.

"If you want I can tell the manager no." It killed me to say it. I wanted so badly to go and hang with the band.

"*You absolutely have to go*," Naomi said eagerly.

"Why?" I was confused. Why did she sound so excited? Maybe she was just happy for me to have friends.

"I want you to help me get my story."

"What?" *Oh no*, I thought. What did she have up her sleeve?

"It's perfect. They won't have their guard up; they won't be rehearsed. They'll be themselves. And if there's any dirt—drugs, girls, booze—then we'll get the scoop."

"But he asked me as a boy not as a boy-band member." I blurted, not liking where this was going. I believed in getting the story, but this felt like too far.

"He *is* a boy-band member, and he *is* a story. Unless he said that it's off the record . . . then it isn't," Naomi said matter-of-factly.

Harmon Holt's words came roaring back to me. *It may be hard to see it now, but the distance between me and you is hard work and opportunity. I am giving you the opportunity*, he had written. *The rest is up to you.*

I didn't know if this is what Mr. Holt meant, but what if, like the Side Effects had said, my chance was coming *now*? If Naomi was giving me a chance to work on a story with her, how could I say no?

I took a deep breath. "Okay," I said.

NINE

The rehearsal session was at their hotel room. I took the elevator up to their top-story suite, muttering to myself about playing it cool the whole way up. When I arrived, their manager was there to greet me. I could hear music coming from the living room. It was the song that I'd heard Henry singing in the studio, and it was beautiful.

So much for keeping my journalistic objectivity.

The boys were sitting on stools and holding mics, Liam singing the lead now.

"You're here," Henry mouthed silently. His face seemed to light up. I was sure that I was imagining it. He probably did that with everyone. It was part of being a teen idol. His job was to make everyone under the age of eighteen fall in love with him. I hated to admit it, but it was working a little.

He smiled again. I forced myself to smile less. Liam suddenly dropped his mic, kicked away from his stool, and plopped down in front in the huge, flat-screen television, grabbing the remote.

"What's his deal?" I asked, looking at Liam. The song still seemed to hang in the air.

Henry didn't seem to hear me. "Hey! We're practicing, man," Henry yelled to Liam.

"Not in front of the enemy," Liam replied, firing up a video game. Manny shrugged and dropped his drumsticks. He went over and picked up a controller.

Henry looked apologetic. "L's not about the press. He's about the music."

"I thought the whole fame and fortune thing just went with the territory," I replied.

"Yeah, but that doesn't mean we have to like it." Henry's face fell, like he was remembering something. "I mean, I know it's what you want to do. No offense."

"None taken," It was my turn to feel bad. He didn't think I was here for the story. He really had invited me just to hang out.

"You want to eat something?" He smiled and grabbed the room service menu.

"Sure." I'd never had room service before, but I guessed they ate that way every night.

Hu ran past, snagging the menu right out Henry's hands. Henry took off after him.

"It's my night to choose," Hu said as Henry chased him around the suite and tackled him to the ground.

"Pizza!" Manny said without taking his eyes off the TV screen.

"Pizza!" Cameron agreed, running his hands through his surfer hair.

"Pizza!" Hu agreed, as if it was his idea to begin with.

"You can have anything you want," Henry said when he returned, slightly out of breath at my side.

"Pizza," I said. I imagined this was what it was like to have brothers—or guy friends.

***

For the next two hours, I played video games with the Side Effects, and for those two hours they seemed like completely normal boys. It was truly unreal.

Their manager walked in, announcing it was time for them to wrap things up: "If you aren't going to practice, you should at least sleep."

Henry walked me to the door.

"That was fun, thanks." For a second, I thought he was going to say more.

But his manager stepped in. "There will be plenty of time for chatting at the party. It's late, so the boys' car will take you home."

"I can get home on my own." I said, not wanting to inconvenience the driver.

"You have to let the car drive you," Henry insisted.

Everyone except Liam shouted their goodbyes. The manager closed the door before I could thank anyone, especially Henry, for possibly the coolest night of my life.

TEN

"You're right. No deep, dark secrets. No drinking, no partying." I dropped my notebooks on my desk with a thud. "They were totally PG. Video games and pizza."

"Boring and useless," Naomi said, disappointed. She leaned against my desk, sipping her coffee and clearly hoping for something more dramatic from me.

I was relieved. I hated disappointing her, but spying on the boys didn't feel right to me either. I could live with boring and useless.

"Well, maybe you'll do better at the party

tonight," she said and walked away before I could protest.

There was no point arguing with her. As far as I was concerned, they had nothing to hide, except maybe Liam's bad manners.

I spent the rest of the day fact-checking and worrying about the party. It was an industry party—whatever that might mean. The boys were planning to perform a new song. The record execs and the press would hear their newest single before it rolled out to radio stations and launched on iTunes a little while later.

I also worried about what I was going to wear.

Tam brought me a cup of coffee and sat down on the edge of the window seat behind my desk.

"I thought I was supposed to bring you coffee . . ." I said.

"*The Rage* has never worked like that. Everyone gets coffee for everyone else, except Holiday. She only drinks that herbal green stuff. It's disgusting."

I laughed.

"How's it going with Naomi?" she asked, crossing her legs under her as if she was settling in to hear some good gossip.

I paused and tried to think of the right words. "She's great. I'm learning so much from her." It was the truth. I just wasn't sure if all that I was learning was good.

"Naomi treats every story exactly the same. Like she's crawling on her belly under razor wire in a war zone and people are shooting at her. But sometimes there's no angle or big secret to uncover. Sometimes a boy band is just a boy band. Keep your head down and try not to get caught in the crossfire."

I nodded. "Thanks, Tam."

Tam got up, still sipping her coffee.

"Tam, one more thing?"

"Anything, hon."

"What do I wear to this thing?"

"Just keep it simple. I mean, definitely no jeans. Black is always good. But don't try too hard. And make sure you still look like you."

I thanked her again and took a big sip of my coffee. I felt better already.

ELEVEN

It was my first industry party. My first New York City party. My first time in a nightclub. The label had rented out the space from the Boom Room, a jazz club on top of the Standard Hotel.

The walls shimmered like the paint itself was made of gold. And there was a ginormous chandelier that dripped down from the ceiling. There was a stage by a wall of windows that looked over downtown Manhattan. A hand-painted sign in front it said, "One Night Only—The Side Effects." The band wasn't on the stage, though.

Dressed up to fit the swanky setting, the Side Effects were working the crowd. Henry looked amazing in a blue suit with a silvery tie and fancy black shoes. He was standing near the stage, talking to some important-looking old guys who were also wearing suits. Probably label execs.

Naomi wasn't dressed up. She was wearing the same outfit she'd been wearing at the office earlier—leather pants and black tank top. But she'd taken off her blazer, revealing toned arms that would make even Michelle Obama jealous. She'd also added a chunky oversized silver necklace. She looked cool without trying.

She had cornered Liam, who did not look at all happy to be talking to her.

I almost felt bad for him, but I made no move to go rescue him.

I looked down at my own outfit. It didn't exactly stand out among all the leather, glitter, and spandex that filled the room, but it was the best I could do. I'd gone beyond simple. A black tank dress that just grazed the knee, my red pumps, and some big hoop earrings. I'd let my hair dry naturally so that it had some waves.

I spotted Henry in the crowd again. His hair was slicked down, and his tie was loose around his neck. He was talking to Cam, who was texting and talking at the same time. Henry laughed as if whatever Cam had said was really funny. I wondered if Henry was thinking about me, if he was wondering whether I would be there.

I reminded myself that the band, that Henry alone, had a gazillion Twitter followers. At the end of the day, I was probably just another fan. I needed to focus on the job—getting the story. I was usually so great at talking to everyone. I had a million questions ready at all times. But Naomi's urge to get dirt on them had made it harder for me to focus. I should have made a beeline for any of the guys and started digging for info. Instead, I headed for the bar, away from the crowds, hoping no one, especially Naomi, would find me there.

"ID please," said the cute and friendly bartender. *Probably an actor hired to be cute and friendly*, I thought.

I automatically looked down at my purse. My driver's license hadn't fit in it. Not that it would have helped anyway.

Next to me a voice said, "He's joking. This bar is just juice."

I looked up, and the bartender nodded and laughed.

"They're serving mocktails," my new neighbor said. He was a cute boy, also about my age, with an accent and hair color that matched Liam's. I was relieved it wasn't Naomi.

"What's a mocktail?" I asked.

"A fake cocktail. Since the band's underage."

The bartender returned with a blue drink in a martini glass. "It's a Side-Car-Effect."

"What's in it?" I asked, lifting the glass to my lips.

"Blueberries, pomegranate . . . and some blue Kool-Aid," the bartender whispered, as if Kool-Aid was a dangerous ingredient.

"We should toast to the band," the blond boy said.

"Cheers." We clinked glasses.

"I'm Lisa."

"Connor. I went to school with Liam back in England. We go way back."

"So are you their biggest fan?" I'd heard of bands traveling with entourages. Maybe this kid's parents let him spent the summer trailing Liam.

"My dad is in the business. He's a record exec. So, since we were in town . . ."

"Cool."

The perks of my dad's job as a cabbie were getting dropped off in the cab at school instead of taking the bus. This kid got to come to New York and hang out with the Side Effects.

Naomi spotted me and waved me over to her. Reluctantly, I said goodbye to Connor and headed over.

Liam pushed past me on the way.

"You okay?" I asked.

"Like you care," he said and continued into the crowd.

"What's his problem?" I asked Naomi when I got to her.

She shrugged. "I think he broke up with Astoria again, but he wouldn't confirm it."

Astoria was an actress who'd starred in one of those kid shows where she played twins—one good and one bad. The show was super popular. And so was Astoria. But since it ended last year, she'd been a hot mess. She was always out too late, had a couple of car accidents, and had stolen a couple of necklaces from photo shoots. Then she started dating Liam—a match made in paparazzi heaven. They broke up and made up on a monthly basis, always in the headlines for one reason or another.

"Is she here?" I asked.

"I wish. I need some color for this story. If she crashed this thing, I would pay her. Not that she needs the money."

Naomi spotted someone that she wanted to talk to across the room. Some lead singer of a band I'd never heard of. He was older than her—probably in his thirties—but he was cute for an older guy. He was wearing almost the exact same outfit that she was—all black, heavy on leather. I trailed along, but I had nothing to add to the conversation. It was like they were speaking another language. This guy's band was popular before I was born, but Naomi knew every song. She sounded less like the tough-as-nails reporter and more like a fan.

The vibe between them had shifted. He was asking her if she wanted to check out his next show at the Bowery. I expected her to shut him down. But instead, Naomi whispered to me, "Go mingle, take notes."

Was Naomi flirting, or was she working on another story? Either way, I took the hint.

She batted her long lashes in the direction of the aging rocker. I walked away as quickly as I could, not wanting to know the answer. I found myself standing next to Hu. He told me about the new T-shirt line that the band was going to design and showed me some of the designs on his phone. He even offered to share them for the article.

I thought they looked cool and really creative. They featured superprofessional drawings depicting the band as cartoon characters. Hu said that the whole band was really into charity work and serious about giving back to the community, especially to school art programs.

As Hu made his way toward the stage for their performance, the images showed up on my tablet and I saved them. But deep down, I knew that there was no way that the charity stuff was going to make Naomi's article. I didn't have the heart to tell him. Maybe a rave review of their music would make the article, though. I crossed my fingers for them as the band made their way up to the stage.

As they were getting set up—Hu on guitar, Cam on bass, Manny on drums, and Henry and Liam in front on the mics—I silently hoped they would blow the crowd, and Naomi, away.

The band played their old hits and the new song that Henry had been working on. The crowd was thrilled. Tam, who was fashionably late, arrived in time to dance on one of the tables with some actor that was a vampire on cable TV. I could never do something like that. But Tam was one of those girls who looked just as comfortable on a tabletop as she did in a board meeting.

And the music was that good. Even Naomi was smiling slightly and tapping her feet to the beat of the music by the end of their set. When they got done, though, she scowled and complained again to the thirtysomething musician. Maybe she was trying to impress him with her skepticism.

Just then, the room got quiet. Naomi had gotten her wish. Astoria was here. She looked exactly like she did in the tabloids. Superlong hair extensions, superlong legs, and superplump lips pouting in Liam's direction. There was a guy on her arm—a guy who was not Liam. A bunch of flashbulbs went off, and people were digging for their camera phones. Naomi glared at me, so I took out my tablet and began to film the encounter, which she would no doubt refer to in her article.

Liam made his way over to Astoria, and they stared at each other a long beat.

What was he going to do?

Liam smiled at Astoria, leaned in, and kissed her on the cheek. Astoria smiled and did the same. She motioned to her companion and introduced the two guys to each other. It all seemed very civil. The room sighed, clearly expecting a train wreck and getting air kisses instead.

Naomi sighed so loud I could feel her breath on my shoulder.

"What does this mean? Are they on-again or off-again?" I asked.

"Do I look like I care? I should be in Iraq, eating MREs and talking to soldiers."

"What's an MRE?" I asked.

Ignoring me, Naomi jotted a few things in her trusty notepad and put her blazer back on again, getting ready to call it a night.

She dismissed me for the evening, pushing a twenty into one of my hands, ordering me to be safe and take a cab, but get a receipt.

She was like that sometimes—motherly. Like she cared what happened to me. But just as quickly, she seemed to remember that she was supposed to have an edge all the time.

I took out my tablet to look up MREs. Meals ready to eat. Totally made sense now.

I headed for the exit, but just as I was leaving a voice came up behind me. "You look pretty." I turned around. It was Henry.

Henry pushed past a couple of waiters carrying trays of desserts to get to me.

"You look pretty, too. I mean, you look good." I blurted. My face felt hot.

"Want to get out of here?" he asked.

***

A few minutes later we were on the roof deck of the hotel. There appeared to be no one else there. It was just us and the view of downtown New York.

"Wow, it's so pretty."

"I agree," he said, but he was looking at my profile and not at the view. I turned to face him.

Henry couldn't possibly like me. This had to be something he did with all the girls.

I'd done my research, though, and Henry hadn't dated anyone famous. But if Naomi was right, then I shouldn't believe what I read about them. The band had an image they were trying to sell, and that included making every girl think that she had a chance with them.

Was I just practice? Or did he hope to get some good press out of all this?

I moved away from him and sat down on one of the fancy white lawn chairs.

"So, do you do this with all the girl reporters?" I blurted.

"Do what?" he asked, sounding innocent.

He sat down beside me, not leaving a lot of space between us.

"Talk to them, take them out on balconies . . ." Even I could tell I sounded ridiculous.

"No, you're the first girl I've ever talked to." He laughed.

I didn't. His eyes softened, like he realized he'd hurt my feelings.

"I never do this with reporters," he said firmly, looking at me in the eye. I believed him.

"Or this," he said, wrapping his hand around mine.

"Or this," he said, and he began to lean in.

Was Henry going to try to kiss me? I told myself to stop thinking and closed my eyes. Nothing happened. I blinked them open. The band's manager was standing in the doorway. Her name was Marnie. She was petite and always looked really pissed off. Or maybe it was just because the first time I met her, Naomi had blackmailed her into continuing the interview sessions. "The car is here, Henry. Do we need to call you one as well, Ms. Harris?" she asked.

Henry and I began to laugh.

TWELVE

In the elevator on the way down to the cars, Henry and I kept laughing. Marnie kept shooting us looks in return, like we were being very bad children.

Henry walked me to my car and opened the door for me, but there was no leaning in. I could see Marnie standing at the door of the other car, supervising as Hu and Cam piled in.

"She's way overprotective. We've gotten burned by the press before. I'll explain to her that you're not really the press."

"But I am really the press. Or at least I want to be. Eventually."

"I didn't mean it like that," he said. "I just meant that you're not here to tear us apart. I mean, the biggest secret we have is that we stayed out last night past curfew playing laser tag in Times Square."

I laughed, feeling really relieved for the first time since Naomi suggested I dig for dirt on the band. There was no dirt to be found. I believed Henry. I could continue my "research" guilt-free.

Before he could close the door for me, I asked, "Can I quote you on that, Mr. Blue?"

He nodded, smiling, and shut the door.

Right away, I realized I'd left my tablet again. I told the driver to wait and went back to retrieve it.

Still on a high from almost kissing Henry, I walked back through the crowd. I could see Marnie in the crowd, too. She was looking for Liam. Maybe he and Astoria had made up after all. Maybe then he would finally be in a better mood. Maybe he was just suffering from a broken heart.

I made my way up to the roof deck. Still remembering Henry leaning in, I paused and took in the view again. But this time I realized that I wasn't alone.

There was a couple kissing—like seriously making out. I immediately recognized Liam's blond shock of hair.

Before I could process what I was seeing, I picked up my tablet and snapped a picture.

When Liam looked up, I hugged the tablet to my chest. He didn't know I'd taken a photo, but he did know I'd seen him. The other guy was Connor. "Connor, go. I'll handle this." Liam said.

Connor opened his mouth in protest. "I met her at the bar. She's cool."

"She's not cool. She's press."

Connor's face fell, like I had completely betrayed him.

He turned and walked away.

I ran off in the other direction, and Liam followed.

Was this my story? My big break. My

opportunity. How important was it to keep his secret? What was he going to do?

THIRTEEN

Liam did the one thing I didn't expect. He begged.

"Please don't tell," he said.

"What about Astoria? Does she know?"

"Astoria and I have been friends forever. She needed to stay in the media. It was a win-win for both of us."

"And Connor?"

"Connor and I have known each other since we were kids. We didn't become more until right before I left for our first tour. He meets me whenever he can. He's not a big fan of hiding out, but he understands."

I suddenly felt very sad. Liam had absolutely everything a kid could want. Looks, money, fame. But he couldn't go public with the person he loved.

Suddenly, it all made sense. Why he was so cagey about being around the press. Why he seemed to hate me from the very beginning. It wasn't about me. It was about keeping his secret. And now, thanks to my stupid tablet, I knew.

"I know I haven't exactly been nice to you. But this is why I haven't wanted press around following me 24-7. It isn't just me on the line. It's the whole band. The Side Effects' fan base is fifteen-year-old girls. What happens if one of us is no longer on the market? If I bring the band down—it's not just my career that's over."

"That's not going to happen," I said, and I believed it. Being gay shouldn't matter.

"Can you promise that? Can you guarantee it? It's too big of a risk for me." He was panicking.

He looked at me for a beat. I didn't answer.

"But then, I guess it's not up to me anymore. It's up to you."

He walked away.

I gripped the railing of the rooftop and looked down at the glittering cityscape. What was I going to do?

FOURTEEN

I didn't sleep, and I didn't text Naomi the picture. When I got downstairs in my dorm, Henry was waiting for me. He was wearing sunglasses and a baseball cap, but I'd know him anywhere.

Liam must have told him all about it.

"I can explain," I said, even though I wasn't sure I could.

I didn't want to know about Liam. I didn't care that he was gay, but it was still a story. How could I not tell Naomi?

"Explain what? I'm the one who should

explain. I'm the stalker who found out where you live from my driver," he said.

'"So why are you here?" I asked.

"I thought we could eat breakfast."

"I'm supposed to go to the office."

"Tell Naomi you're with me. I bet she'll be thrilled."

He was right. I picked up my cell and made the call. Sure enough, Naomi told me to go for it. "*Get the story*," she whispered before we hung up. Little did she know—I already had one.

We walked outside. I expected to see the SUV, but it wasn't there.

He pulled down his baseball cap a little further and grabbed my hand.

An hour-long subway ride later, we stepped onto the boardwalk at Coney Island.

"This is where you wanted to take me for breakfast?"

Anyone could recognize him here. He could be mobbed. There could be paparazzi or reporters. Technically, *I* was a reporter. Not that I was acting like one.

"They have the best funnel cakes in the world."

He paid for our tickets and our funnel cakes. We people-watched and talked while eating the sugary powdered cakes that he had dragged me all the way out here to eat.

After we ate, we rode the Cyclone. He held my hand the whole time while my other hand gripped the safety bar.

After we'd ridden all the rides, we took a stroll down the boardwalk. We ate cotton candy and pretzels.

Eventually, we found ourselves back on the boardwalk, looking at the water. The summer crowd was there, but thankfully no one seemed to notice the star among them. After a while, he lost the sunglasses and I could see his big brown eyes.

"My mom used to take me for breakfast here once a year. She'd write school a note saying I was sick, and we'd spend the whole day here."

I'd almost forgotten that New York was his hometown. When he was on stage, he seemed like he belonged to the world. But right now he seemed like a regular boy.

"Why here?"

"I was a pretty weird kid. Super serious about wanting to sing. I would ride the train into the city for auditions every week. Mom brought me here so she could remind me what it was like to be a kid and have fun."

"When you were a kid . . . you're so old now," I teased.

"Sometimes I feel really old. But not here."

"And now you brought me. How would Mom feel about that?"

"She'd love it. She hates the rollercoasters."

I bit my lip, realizing something.

"Is that why you brought me here? Because I'm no fun?"

"No, of course not, Lisa . . ."

He drifted off, and I panicked. Was I a project? A fixer-upper or something?

"What you said the other day about working so hard to get what you want—I get that," he said gently. "You can get where you're going and still be a kid. Have fun. Have a life. Go to

Coney Island for breakfast."

I didn't say anything, but I was listening. He was different than I'd thought. I guess when you see someone on a poster and on TV, you forget that they are real. I hadn't talked this much or this way with anyone in my whole life. It didn't get any more real than that.

I still couldn't look at him, even though I could feel his eyes on me.

"I'm better at asking questions than at answering them," I said simply.

"That's okay, we don't have to talk," Henry said, looking out at the water.

And just like that, him saying that I didn't have to, made me want to tell him everything. I told him about school—about not having many friends there. He told me about how he lucked out with the band, how they had become his friends and family. I felt a twinge of jealousy for that. I'd never had that. But I did have my dad, I told him. Dad, who was strong, loyal, funny, and worked night shifts so that he could be home every day after school for dinner.

"He sounds great," Henry said.

"My dad would never do this. I have perfect attendance."

"No one has perfect attendance unless they're like five."

"Well, I do."

"That explains a lot," he said lightly. "I work hard, I play hard," he added.

"That's kind of what I was afraid of." I let go of his hand. The spell was broken. I remembered that he was Henry Blue, famous boy-band star, not a normal boy. And while I didn't think I was getting played, I didn't think that this could last either. Maybe not today, maybe not tomorrow, but sometime soon, he would remember that we weren't part of the same world. It was better to hurt a little now than a lot later.

"I didn't mean it like that."

"You must have a different girl in every city," I mumbled.

"I don't. I could—Hu does. And Cam. But I don't." He sighed, disappointed.

"Why not?"

"I've dated a lot, but no one serious. I had a girlfriend before all this. She broke up with me because I was spending too much time with my music. So now, when I date someone, I don't know if they're dating me for me or for the fame. And with the schedule and everything, it's always hard. But now . . ."

"Now what?"

He didn't answer with words. He kissed me. For split second all I could think was that I was kissing Henry Blue. The Henry Blue. But seconds later I was kissing just Henry—the normal, good guy who wanted to eat funnel cakes with me at Coney Island and learn about my life.

***

There was more kissing on the way back to my dorm. He got a call from the manager telling him that he was late for rehearsal. When the car stopped, he kissed me again.

"I'll text you when I'm done."

I got out of the back of the SUV, almost dizzy from the kissing.

After I closed the door, I remembered the tablet. I opened it again.

"I think I need to get a leash for that thing."

But Henry wasn't smiling. He was holding the tablet in his hands, staring me down like something was very, very wrong.

FIFTEEN

"You forgot this." Henry was looking at me like he didn't know me.

He was holding my tablet in his hand. My stomach twisted. I knew what was on it before I could see it. He tilted it in my direction. The picture of Liam and Connor was on the screen.

"*I* wasn't spying. It just turned on on its own," he said, as if there were any question as to who had the moral high ground here.

"I can explain," I blurted, knowing full well that I couldn't really.

"You spent the entire day with me while you were carrying this around. Were you hoping to gather some information on Liam? Was that what today was about?"

"You asked me out today, remember? *You* showed up here," I defended myself.

His eyes were cold now.

"It's not your secret to tell," he said simply.

Now I was angry. "I'm a journalist. This could make my career."

"Yeah? And what about Liam? Do you care what happens to him?"

"He's a public figure," I answered. And why should I care? He'd been so awful to me from the second I met him.

"So he doesn't have feelings? He doesn't have rights?"

"He doesn't get to have privacy. I'm sorry. It's not personal." My voice sounded so cold it almost didn't sound like mine anymore. It reminded me of Naomi.

"It is personal. And if you don't see that, you're not the person I thought you were."

He stormed off, his cell phone already in

hand, ready to do damage control.

"Liam, hey. Pick up, please."

I watched him go. I didn't have anything to say to stop him.

SIXTEEN

"I need something more than Henry is a really good kisser," Naomi whispered to me as I walked into the studio.

The Side Effects were already setting up behind the glass.

Henry was staring straight ahead, like I wasn't standing right in front of him.

Liam was looking at me, his eyes bleary and red, as if he hadn't slept.

I did that to him.

"Let's try something new today," Henry said to the band. "Can you guys follow?" He turned back to the band.

Manny nodded and held his drumsticks tighter.

I thought you were new
I thought you were true
Now I'm blue
Because you're like the rest
Trying to tear down the best
I thought you were new
Now I'm blue
Now we're just through

Henry sang with his eyes closed.

Ouch. Every girl wants someone to write a song about them . . . just not this song.

I deserved it. But it still hurt to hear.

Naomi looked from me to Henry and back again.

She knew something was up.

The rest of the band didn't seem to notice. Manny had found just the right beat. Hu was leaning into his guitar, finding the right melody. Cam was catching up on the bass. They were all getting into the Henry-hates-Lisa song.

Naomi's head was moving to the beat. "Now that's passion," she said. Was she trying to get a reaction from me?

Liam called five, and the other boys congratulated Henry on the killer track.

"How'd you come up with it? It's way different than your other stuff," Naomi asked, recorder in hand.

"I don't know, it just kind of hit me out of nowhere like I was sucker punched," he said, choosing his words carefully. He didn't name me, but he made sure I knew exactly what he was talking about.

"Well, you should get punched more often." Naomi smiled.

"What?"

"You sounded great—like you were singing about something you actually cared about."

"Well, I don't care anymore," he stammered, and rushed away.

"Sure sounded like you do," Naomi mumbled.

She finished jotting down her notes and turned to leave. "When you're ready to tell me what you have on our boys, I'll be back at the office," she whispered.

I felt the tears stinging somewhere behind my eyes, and I willed them not to come. I began to gather my things, but Naomi stopped me. "Stay, watch the rest of the session. I have to run a couple of errands on the way back to the office."

Naomi let herself out of the studio.

When I turned back around, Liam was there.

"What are you going to do?"

"I don't know," I said. I was being honest, but Liam looked like he didn't believe me. He thought I was playing with him. With his life.

When I looked up, Henry was standing in the door.

"Then we don't have anything to talk about," said Henry. He turned his back on me, and the two of them headed back into the soundproof room.

SEVENTEEN

Back at the office, I went to my desk and waited for Naomi find me there. Instead, I ran into Holiday.

"How is your internship going? Are you enjoying your time with Naomi?"

Tam had asked me the same question days ago. This time I could answer without hesitating.

"She's teaching me everything she knows."

Holiday smiled brightly.

"Any questions for me?"

"How did you get your first big story?"

"Well, I was a lot older than you. And the story kind of found me."

The story about Liam had found me, too. Did that mean I was supposed to tell it?

"How's that?"

"I was on assignment for this beauty magazine I was working at, and while I was there covering a fashion shoot for an actress, the hotel next door got bombed. I had to make a decision: run for my life, or go cover it. So I covered it."

"Wow, that's huge."

"*The Rage* walks that line between the human-interest stuff and just the human stuff. I get the best of both worlds. One day it's how Beyoncé and Jay-Z have changed since they had the baby, and the next day it's how you can help save babies in Malawi. I think that there's room to cover both kinds of stories."

After Holiday walked away, I stared at my blank computer screen.

Finally, I knew what I had to do. I took a deep breath and began to write.

Naomi approached my desk about an hour later.

I handed her the printout of what I wrote.

She read it over. When she was done, she rolled her eyes like she was a teenager and not a twentysomething.

"I think you have something better."

"Then your hunch is wrong. This is all I have."

"They're not going to thank you, you know. This story could have been your ticket. A month from now they'll be back on tour, living their lives, not giving a crap about you."

I didn't say anything.

"Crushes die. But the article would have lived forever."

"But I would have to live with myself."

She left the paper I'd written on my desk. I had picked it up, ready to throw it in the trash, when Tam came by.

"Let me read it, at least."

I shrugged and handed it to her.

EIGHTEEN

The Side Effects were back on the road now—a different city every day. I didn't hear back from Henry when I texted him to apologize.

I followed the band online. Like Naomi predicted, they all looked happy, like they'd moved on. I searched for clips of Henry on YouTube singing the song that he wrote about me. But from what I could tell, he never sang it again. Maybe he didn't even have the energy to hate me anymore. I wondered if he ever thought of me at all.

When the article came out, I made myself

read it. It certainly wasn't a love letter to the band, but Naomi didn't trash them either.

The band shows promise. I heard them perform a hate song that was better than any of their love songs. Most people will probably think it's some shallow song about Liam's ex, who breaks up with him on a weekly basis. But I think it was the most honest thing I've heard them play. It probably won't make their album, but it should. When they stop being who they think the world wants them to be and start being who they really are . . . I'd like a front-row seat at that concert.

Naomi's writing was still good, even without leaking some huge secret.

Naomi got her wish to go on an overseas assignment again. She was in South Korea, covering a story about the soldiers who guarded the border there. It was just the kind of thing that she lived for. I picked up my phone to text her about the article, to tell her that I thought it was good and to thank her for the chance to learn from her.

I dropped the magazine when I reached for the phone. It fell open to a bonus page about the

Side Effects. *An extra? I didn't know about that*, I thought.

I picked it up and found pictures of Hu's T-shirts and *my* article, "The Secret Life of the Side Effects," lining the two-page spread—the article I'd given to Naomi to read. It was all about the charities that each boy in the band spent time working with. But how did it get in the magazine?

I went to see Tam.

"I gave it to Holiday. She thought it was well written and an angle that we hadn't yet seen about the boys. Congratulations."

I hugged Tam. She did this for me? And Holiday actually liked it?

This had to be my breakthrough.

My first byline!

NINETEEN

A few days before the end of my internship, I read that they were back. I wasn't expecting to hear from them, so I was beyond surprised when I found Liam in the lobby of my dorm.

A few minutes later, we plopped down on the bed in my room.

"Thank you for not telling."

"It wasn't my secret to tell." I said, repeating Henry's words and meaning them.

"Hu's over the moon about the article about the graphic tees. He retweeted it. You're going to have a gazillion followers now."

I didn't know about the retweet. It probably wasn't the same as having a byline with Naomi, but it felt good.

"What made you do it—or not do it? No offense, you seemed like the story-at-any-cost type, like Naomi," he said suddenly, searching my eyes for an answer, like he couldn't figure me out.

"I guess I'm not exactly like Naomi after all. Besides, you should know better than anyone that first impressions can be totally off. Like, when I met you I thought you were a total jerk."

"I was a total jerk to you. Sorry."

I shrugged. "I get it. But for what it's worth, I don't think you have anything to hide. It's 2014. Don't you think the world is ready for you?" He was silent, thinking.

"How's Henry?" I asked, not able to go another minute without knowing.

"Why don't you ask him yourself? We're having a private concert tonight. No press. Just friends and family."

"And you want me to come?"

"It'll be fun."

TWENTY

When I entered the hotel room, the band was already playing. It was a new song, and it sounded more grown-up. When they finished, I hung back.

I tried not to stare at Henry, but I couldn't help it.

Hu came over to see me first. He was wearing one of his T-shirts. He pulled it out from his chest proudly.

"Have you checked your Twitter? You're going to totally blow it."

I shook my head.

Hu pulled out his phone and clicked on my name. Twenty *thousand* followers. I'd only had a hundred yesterday.

"Thanks, Hu!"

Hu spotted Henry coming our way and moved on to talk to his parents.

I didn't know what to say to Henry. I didn't know what he was going to say to me.

"I got your texts. I needed some time. . . . It was cool of you not to run with the story."

I nodded. The band's manager, Marnie, cleared her throat. Henry hadn't called or written or texted all month. Whatever we were or whatever we could have been was over the second I took that stupid picture.

"We should get seats," he said. "Liam has something he wants to announce."

TWENTY-ONE

Liam took his place in front of the room. It wasn't a who's-who of Hollywood. It was strictly friends and family, all of their parents, and a few kids our age, including Connor and Astoria.

Connor caught me looking at him and smiled. Astoria was smiling, bright, happy, and just for Liam. She had the whole world convinced that she was this spoiled witch, but at the end of the day she was true friend to him. She *was* a really good actress.

Liam announced that he was gay. He

explained that he hadn't wanted to risk the band's popularity by telling the truth.

Henry got up and patted him on the shoulder.

Manny gave him a hug.

Hu pretended to be not at all surprised and did the same.

Cam stood to the side for a minute, as if he was still trying to figure out the words that Liam had said. Then he moved in to give Liam a bear hug and said, "It doesn't matter to me that you're gay. Just don't ever lie to us again, man."

Liam beamed, looking half-surprised and half-confused by the warm response.

***

The rest of Liam's family and friends circled him for hugs and kind words.

I felt myself tear up. I decided it was time for me to go.

I hadn't ruined anything for Liam or the band. I'd only ruined things for me and Henry. I began to back out of the room, but someone caught up with me. I was hoping it would be

Henry, but it was Liam.

"That was so brave," I said. "And I promise it's off the record."

"I don't think I would have done it if it weren't for you."

"I bet you would have."

"I'm not ready to tell the world yet, but when I am—I'd like to tell you. On the record."

"I'd be honored."

I hugged him and began to walk away again.

This time a voice stopped me.

It was Henry's, and he was singing. I turned around.

I thought you were new
I thought you were true
Now I'm blue
Because I miss you
Now I'm blue
I hope we're not just through

I felt myself melt as he closed the gap between us.

"I thought you couldn't trust me anymore," I said.

"You didn't publish the article when you could have. I know what it meant to you."

"I shouldn't have even thought about it. The second I saw the way you looked at me when you found that picture, I realized what a mistake it would have been. I should have realized it sooner."

"But you did realize it. That's what matters."

TWENTY-TWO

Dear Mr. Holt,

I have just completed my summer at The Rage. *I can't thank you enough for the experience.*

I had a plan for the summer: get my first byline. But I ended up getting a lot more than that.

I always knew that I wanted to be a reporter when I grew up, but I never knew what kind of reporter I wanted to be until this summer.

I had the honor of working with one of the

best journalists in the field, Naomi Jax. She puts the story first—before everything. Two years ago, I read her amazing article on children fighting in the war in Sudan. Her words are what made me want to pursue journalism. In some ways, I want to be just like her when I grow up. In others ways, I hope to make my own path.

Being a good journalist means that you have to be objective. But I want to make sure that I remain a good person, too. Journalism can put your goodness at stake by requiring you to question and challenge people.

I always knew I wasn't supposed to change how a story comes out. What I didn't know was how much the story could change me.

Next summer, I'm going back to The Rage, *where I hope to learn more about what it takes to be a great journalist . . . and maybe even publish another byline or two.*

Thank you,
Lisa Harris

ABOUT THE AUTHOR

D. M. Paige attended Columbia University and her first internship eventually led her to her first writing job at *Guiding Light*, a soap opera. She writes and lives in New York City.

COUNTERATTACK

SOUTHSIDE HIGH

check out all the books in the

SURVIVING SOUTH SIDE

collection